# BORN to be KIND

# Dedicated to my little girl.
# May you always choose kindness.

## This book belongs to

_____

Hi, I'm Kate, and my favorite part of the day
Is heading to the park with my mum to play.

I love all the slides,
seesaws and swings,
The rungs to climb
and other exciting things.

The joy in the park has only just begun,
I'm so excited to play in the afternoon sun.

Munching a tasty sandwich,
I sat near the pool

And, there, I saw a lovely kitten
wearing a pink jewel.

Her eyes were so bright and green,
She was such a lovely, kitty queen.

Mum, look! The kitten is playing near the puddle.

She's splashing water so joyfully and in a muddle!

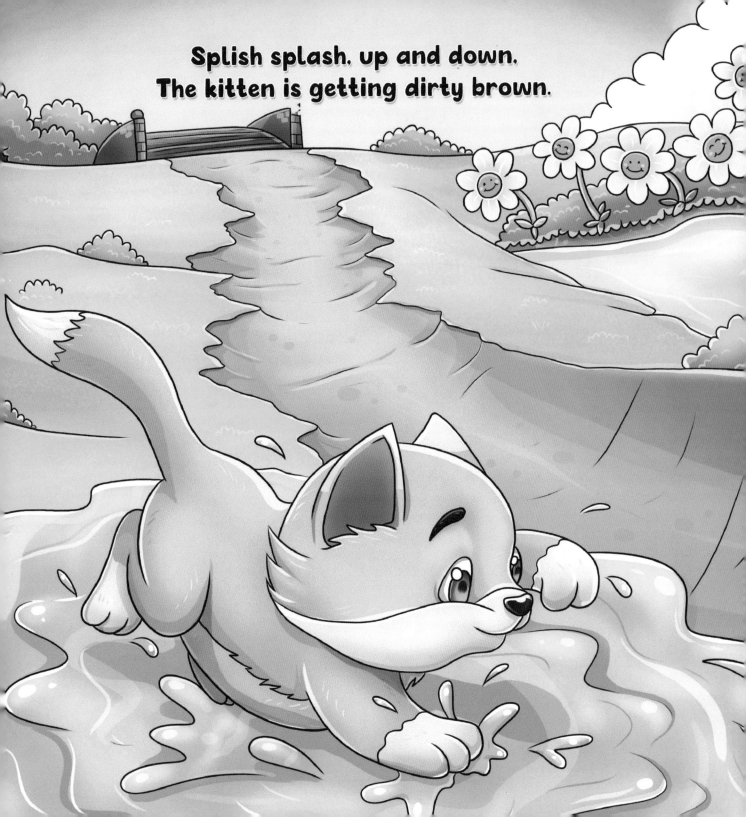

Splish splash, up and down,
The kitten is getting dirty brown.

It's now rolling on the ground,
around in the dirt,

Splashing water
all over my favorite T-shirt.

I looked behind the swing and a big pile of clay,
Hey, kitty! Please come out and don't hide away.

And then I found her,
playing by an old tree,

Jumping over the piles of leaves,
one, two, three!

Suddenly, she jumped so high from the big tree,

Falling down on the ground and bending her knee.

Hey, mom! The kitten fell down, she's badly hurt,

We need to pick her up and get some aid first.

We bring kitty to the hospital,
put her on a bed,
Mum called the nurse as I gently
pat her head.

Nurse puts the bandage on kitty's knee, round and round.

But kitty got ticklish and made some sort of laughing sound.

Your kitten will be alright soon, that's what the nurse said.

You can take her home and feed some meat and some bread.

Soon after mum called a cab and we went home.
I cleaned the kitty's fur with a gentle hair comb.

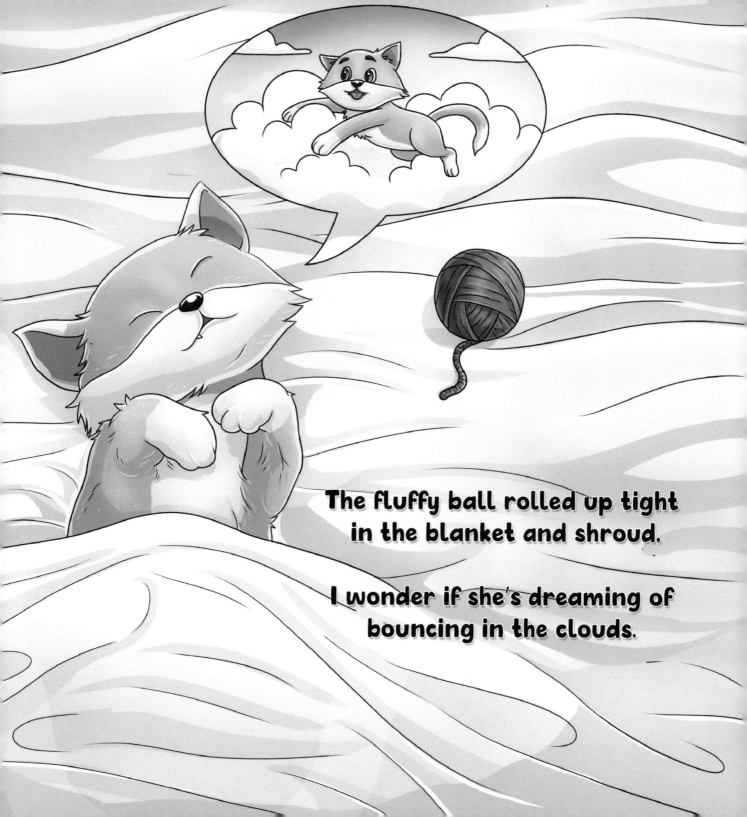

The fluffy ball rolled up tight
in the blanket and shroud,

I wonder if she's dreaming of
bouncing in the clouds.

Hey, Kate, that was such a lovely act of kindness, my mum said,

You helped an injured kitten, and she bent down to pat my head.

We should spread kindness in each and every place,
Towards any human or an animal, and fill all the space.

Your little acts of goodwill and smiles
Fill the gaps with happiness, it travels miles.

Spread comfort and joy in every possible way
And love yourself and others every day.

Listening to mom filled me with happiness in the inside,
Kindness is something I will always do, I firmly decide.

No matter if someone is big or if they are small.
I will carry it day and night by helping them all.

Happy to see her looking all fine,
I joyfully wiggle.

I thanked mum for taking care of
the kitten and we giggle.

I went to bed, tired, and slept until dawn
Hoping the cat will be fine in the morn.

Aha! I've found her, in the yard, happily having a run,
Her wounds healed up nicely as if there were none.

Up! Up! the kitten is jumping high in the sky,
Chasing after a butterfly that flutters up high.

There is a sparkle in my beautiful pet kitty's eyes.
Curiously watching the butterfly high in the skies.

I watched the kitten all day and didn't once budge
And mom baked my favourite cake, chocolate fudge.

Unable to catch the butterfly,
the little kitty sadly took a break

And we sat and laughed together and
enjoyed our favourite cake.

# Let's take kitty to the Hospital.

Printed in Great Britain
by Amazon